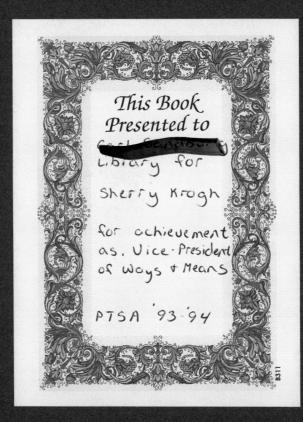

This Book
Presented to
~~Carl Sandburg~~
Library for

Sherry Krogh

for achievement
as, Vice-President
of Ways & Means

PTSA '93 '94

B311

Cabbage Rose

by M. C. Helldorfer
illustrated by Julie Downing

Bradbury Press   New York

Maxwell Macmillan Canada   Toronto
Maxwell Macmillan International
New York   Oxford   Singapore   Sydney

Bradbury Press
Macmillan Publishing Company
866 Third Avenue
New York, NY 10022

Maxwell Macmillan Canada, Inc.
1200 Eglinton Avenue East
Suite 200
Don Mills, Ontario M3C 3N1

Macmillan Publishing Company is part of the Maxwell
Communication Group of Companies.

First American edition
Printed and bound in Singapore
10 9 8 7 6 5 4 3 2 1

The text of this book is set in Centaur.
The illustrations are rendered in watercolor.
Book design by Julie Quan

LIBRARY OF CONGRESS CATALOGING-IN-PUBLICATION DATA
Helldorfer, Mary Claire, date–
Cabbage Rose / by M. C. Helldorfer ; illustrated by Julie Downing.
— 1st ed.
p. cm.
Summary: While painting pictures for the royal family,
plain Cabbage falls in love with the prince and decides to use her
magic paintbrush to increase her own chances.
ISBN 0-02-743513-X
[1. Fairy tales.] I. Downing, Julie, ill. II. Title.
PZ8.H367Cab 1993
[E] — dc20 91-9833

For Jean and Harry, with love
— M.C.H.

To Jeffrey and Jamie
— J.D.

Have you seen how, each day, the plain
yellow sun paints the world in wonderful colors?
I met a girl who could do that. She was an artist,
and she painted skies and rivers and children's
faces as perfect as roses. But the girl herself was
plain, and her brothers called her Cabbage.

Cabbage lived and worked at her brothers' inn on the road that wound through King's Forest. Many people stopped by this inn: ladies on their way to meet the prince; rich men who hoped that their daughters would win the prince's heart; and once, on a half-moon night, a magician.

He arrived after all the other guests were in bed. The brothers, too, for they were a lazy pair. Only Cabbage was awake, painting in a room alight with candles.

She sprang up to help the man, but the magician told her, "I will rest here." Then he sat to watch her paint.

The next morning he left before Cabbage awoke. She found the blanket with which she had covered him, neatly folded. The pot of tea she had made him was empty. Beside it lay a new paintbrush.

Cabbage carried the magician's brush in her pocket all day, and when her work was finally done, she began to paint again—roses, like those a beautiful lady might bring to the prince.

But when she touched her new brush to the canvas, something strange and wonderful happened.

The petals she painted unfolded. Stems and leaves twisted free. The fragrance of roses filled the room. Whatever the girl painted became real.

In a few days' time the inn was crowded with curious people. Under her brothers' watchful eyes, Cabbage painted small gifts for the guests and toys for the children. Others tried the brush, but only Cabbage could paint with magic.

"Only plain girls need magic," her brothers jeered. They drove away the crowds and barred the shutters and doors.

"Paint me a pearl," the older one demanded. "Make it the biggest in the world."

Trembling a little, Cabbage picked up her brush. A pearl large and luminous as the rising moon rolled off her easel.

Then the other brother cried out, "Paint me two diamonds, as big as windows!"

She did, and she painted chandeliers like ice fountains, rugs soft and colorful as peacock feathers, cups twisted with silver, and chains of gold. The more she painted, the more the brothers wanted, until, too weary to go on, Cabbage fell down by her easel.

She awoke alone. Quickly she painted a bag and a cape, and on the shutters, stars, moonlight, and trees. Then, gathering her paints and brushes, she climbed through the window into a summer night.

Cabbage followed the forest road without stopping until she reached the marketplace of the king's city. It was noontime, and farmers' stalls were filled with good things to eat, but she had no money.

For cheese and bread, she painted a farmer's face on the side of his wagon; for a bolt of strong cloth, she painted a proud weaver; for a room of her own, a portrait of the weaver's children.

In that room she hid her magic brush, afraid that her brothers would hear of her. Every morning she went to the market to paint. The farmers greeted her cheerfully, and children gathered close to watch her work. Cabbage was happier than she had ever been.

Then came the summons from the palace.

The prince said to the artist, "My father and I have heard of your skill. If you will paint twelve pictures for our great hall, we shall reward you richly."

So Cabbage began her work and the prince came to watch. He came the next day, and the next, bringing her little surprises— wildflowers, smooth stones, a shell from a faraway sea. The prince was filled with wonder by the artist's pictures. While she painted he told her tales, some true and some magical. Once he told a tale of love. Cabbage blushed, and he called her Rose.

On the day the last painting was finished, Cabbage cried. She did not want to leave, for she had fallen in love with the prince.

In her room she took out her magic brush. Standing before a mirror, she painted a face as lovely as those she had seen at the palace, a dress prettier than any she had ever worn. With the last, soft touch of her brush, her own dress changed. She smiled, and the perfect lady in the mirror smiled back. Slipping her brush in a bag, Cabbage hurried to the palace.

The guards did not know her.
The king welcomed Cabbage as a stranger.
The prince greeted her, then turned away.

So Cabbage drew out her magic brush and painted jewels that glittered like a handful of stars. "Tell me what you wish for," she told the prince. "I can paint it real."

"Then paint Cabbage Rose," the prince replied. "For the world is plain without her."

Cabbage broke the brush in two.
She stood before the court, herself again.

Some kind of magic ended then, but the people say another
kind began. In the marketplace they celebrated Cabbage's return.
The children gathered close to her, laughing and talking while she
painted. No one could keep them still, except the prince, when he
told a gentle tale about a girl named Cabbage Rose.